GW00503818

THE
XXXX
FILES

David Lines was born in Nottingham. He has worked as a journalist, on local radio and is presently a creative copywriter for an advertising agency. He lives in York and is married to Samantha.

John Abbott was born in Toronto, Canada and lives in N. Yorkshire

David Lines gives it up for:

Robin Jarvis,
Chris and Phil Lines, The Floyd,
Andrew Carrick,
Clive Frayne,
The inspirational Richard Reynolds,
Candia McWilliam, Mt Wendell,
Ludy Ridley,
My Mum,
Steve Jackson,
And for Samantha, always for Samantha.

John: Big thanks to the following for their continued friendship and ideas: Nathan Beer, Andy Garland, Paul Gill, Dom, Mark Nicholson, Matt Watson, Rick Lynch, Huw Spacey. Big shout outs to: Random House & Arrow Publishing, Ma, Pa, Bev, Chris & Josh, my girlfriend Sue, Chris Edwards, Jim Smart, Rootabager Si & Ali, Fx1, Nihlist, Matthew Smith (for JSW & MM) Shuddering zombies and the sallow grey humanoids with almond-shaped eyes who perform insidious experiments on my larynx.

jon@alien23.demon.co.uk

THE XXXX FILES

David Lines
John Abbott

ARROW

Published in the United Kingdom in 1996 by Arrow Books

2 4 6 8 10 9 7 5 3 1

Copyright © 1996 by David Lines
Illustrations © 1996 by David Lines and John Abbott

The right of David Lines and John Abbott to be identified as the authors
of this work has been asserted by them in accordance with the Copyright,
Designs and Patents Act, 1988

This book is sold subject to the condition that it shall not by way of trade
or otherwise, be lent, resold, hired out, or otherwise circulated without
the publisher's prior consent in any form of binding or cover other than
that in which it is published and without a similar condition including
this condition being imposed on the subsequent purchaser

First published in the United Kingdom in 1996 by Arrow Books

Arrow Books Limited
Random House UK Ltd, 20 Vauxhall Bridge Road, London SW1V 2SA

Random House Australia (Pty) Limited
20 Alfred Street, Milsons Point, Sydney
New South Wales 2061, Australia

Random House New Zealand Limited
18 Poland Road, Glenfield, Auckland 10, New Zealand

Random House South Africa (Pty) Limited
PO Box 2263, Rosebank 2121, South Africa

Random House UK Limited Reg. No. 954009

A CIP catalogue record for this book is available from the British Library

Printed and bound in Hong Kong

ISBN 0 09 918182 7

"Tell me about it", said Guthrex,
"..they all look the same to me..."

Free study Periods were proving pointless for Zuncan, as h
student flatmates seemed to lack some commitment...

Ever since Joob's brother went out with friends cruising for chicks at Roswell, his mother had always been reluctant to let him borrow the stationwagon. Today didn't help matters...

As a government scientist, Zarin could distort the very fabric of time and space using high gravity generators and anti-matter, but programming a VCR was beyond his current realm of understanding.

When Argox's landing gear dropped off,
man's evolution speeded-up somewhat...

FIRST CONTACT: The long awaited historic meeting between both worlds ended, when FBI Agent Burns failed to show up...

The Research Team hadn't quite got their act together for the landing party's discreet integration into society....

"Houston, we have a problem...."

"I don't give a shit whether this Lucan guy is a Lord - he's mine and I'm keepin' him!"

"That's the bastard, third from the left!
- I'd know that guy anywhere..."

"I'm sorry to tell you that on this occasion, you've been unsuccesful in passing your driving test." The cereal crops grown on this particular planet proved an ideal test area for emergency stops.

"What's that rubbish they've built?"
"Well - you pay peanuts, you get primates..."

After hiding the remote, placing loose change down the back of the sofa and removing one sock from the tumble dryer, Phobos waited to observe the humans....

Zarin had hours of fun teasing the humans.
He was always amazed at how gulible they were...

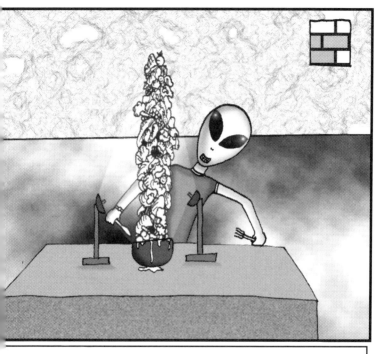

Garlan used his anti-gravity generator to exploit the
"All the salad you can cram" offer at his local 'Happy Pizza'....

"WATCH OUT FOR THE FAT BLOKE!!!"

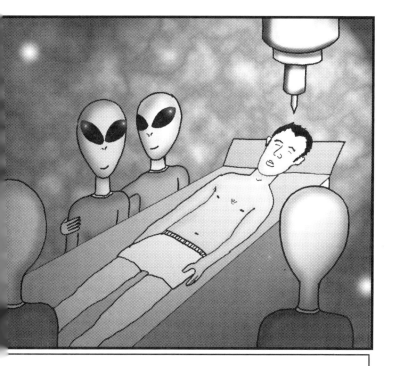

Maz and Brynja found it increasingly difficult to keep their office romance a secret....

"There you go - I told you I used to be a big star!"

The Blur/Oasis debate had started
to get out of hand...

"My other ship is a 1732b Hyper Distorter"

"Call off the invasion, these humans
are 7 foot tall with ....GIANT EARS!!!"

Vango finally accepted that, without ears,
he could never look cool....

Take That's break-up hit Nathos hard....

In years to come, Armus would regret
his 'Alien/Sheep' hybrid experiments...

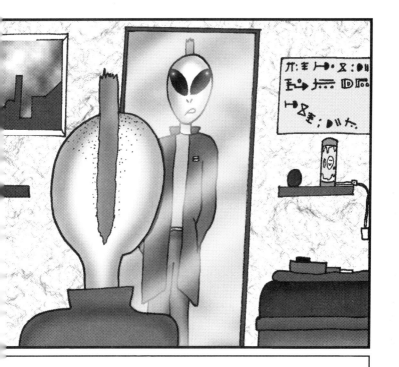

"You talkin' to me?".

"Cadet Bjerk, your mission is to integrate into the heart of youth culture..."

The 'Doorstep Challenge' was about to be
taken to another dimension....

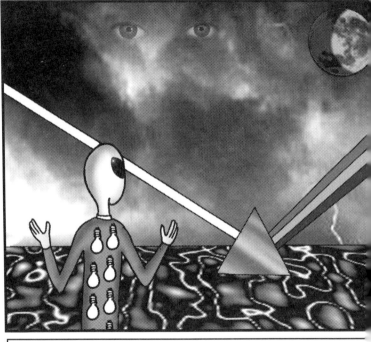

Zarin's obsession with 'The Floyd' was beginning
to concern his friends...

"You know what they say - big ship, small dick."

"Buck Rogers..... Schmuck Rogers!"

1970's game designers were taken more seriously when
the Greys began invading Earth in their warships....

"What are these humans...... bastard midgets?"

Run for your lives, everyone - the bitch is back!!!!!!!"

"Coast's clear! you can come out now - they've gone"

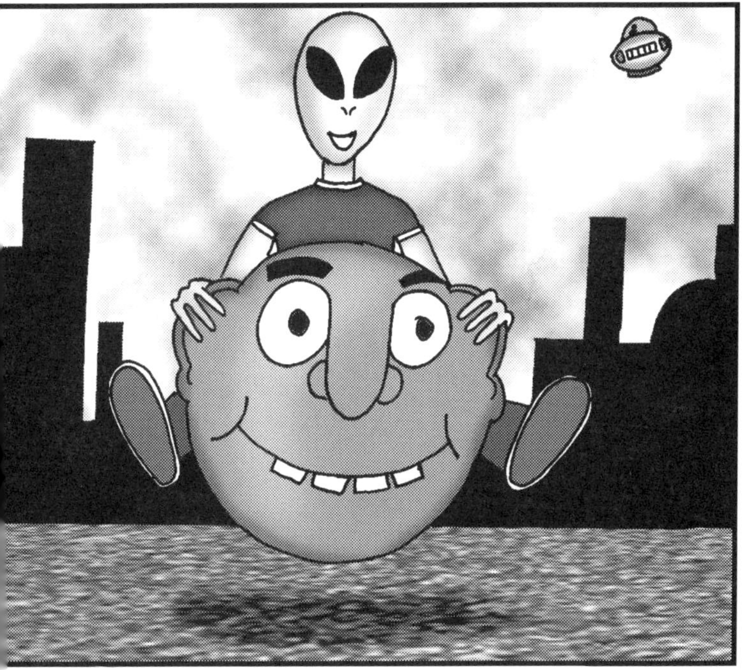

EARTH HOPPER

Being an expert in the chaos theory,
Gilzad knew he'd win this simple human game.
The large hand was something of a surprise, though...

The kids were kept amused for hours with
Grandad's old war stories...

Agent Zuldur knew that his Government were abducting humans from earth - proving it was the difficult part...

Sad, isn't it? how Nigel really believed that
one day he'd spot a UFO...

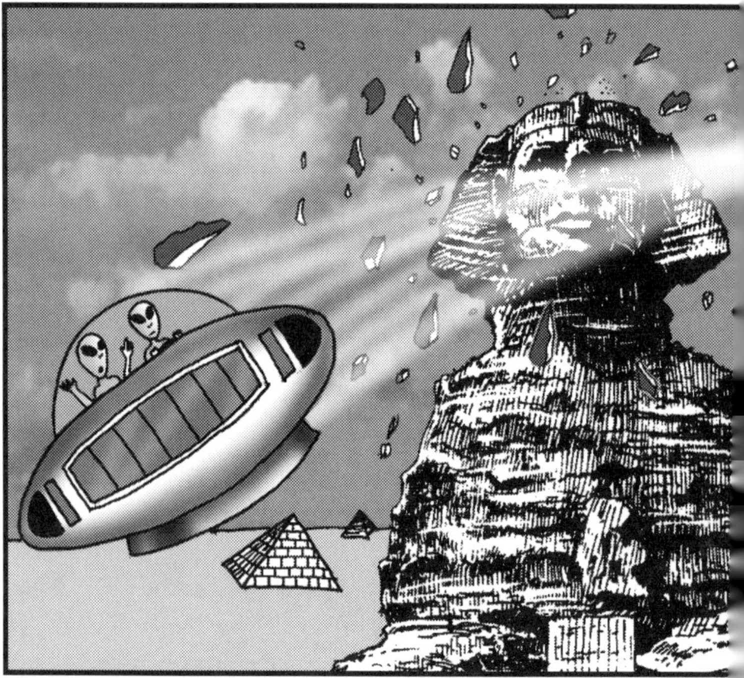

"JEEZ! - That was close..."

SUBLIMINAL INTEGRATION....

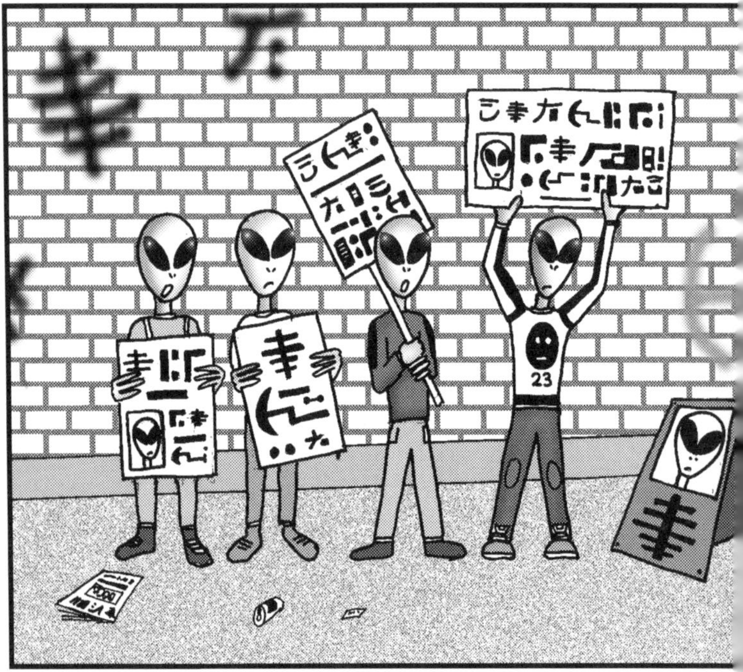
23

GREY RIGHTS ACTVISTS.

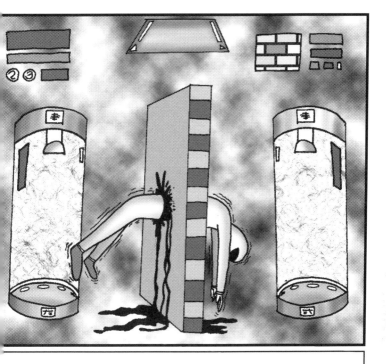

Zarin's experiments in Dimensional Shifting
still needed some fine tuning...

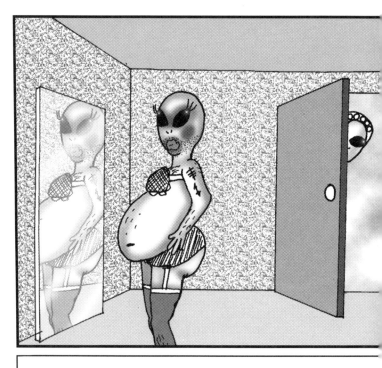

Fizzard's double life came to an abrupt halt when his
wife arrived home early from work...

Noel had bitten off more than he could chew with this
particular unsuspecting household...

"Typical. You wait for hours and then
three come along at once...."

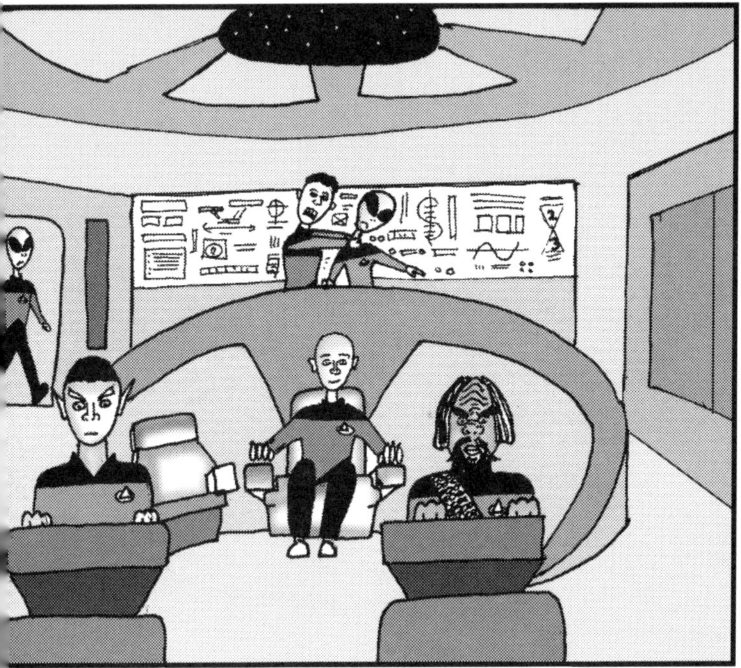

When the Greys were finally accepted into Starfleet,
old human prejudices still remained...

"After everything we've done - he makes one big Spielberg movie and doesn't even bother to 'phone home!"

"Well, what the hell _did_ you think they were made out of?"

The death of Zelvis was far from unexpected...

"What did I tell you...? These things need servicing every 2000 light years!"

"Weird... no property section."

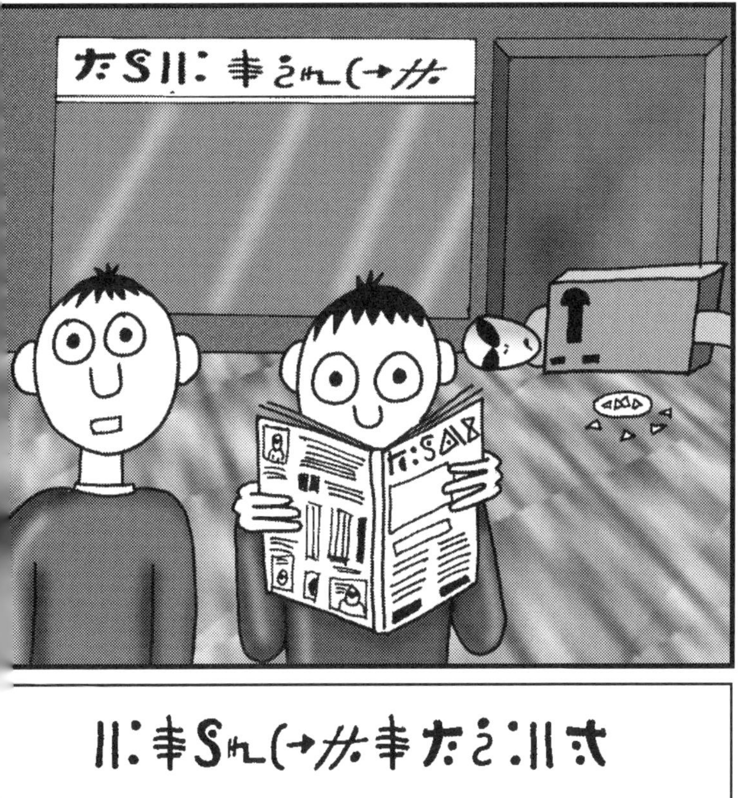

It was at that precise moment in time that Zarin deeply regretted spilling this guy's pint...

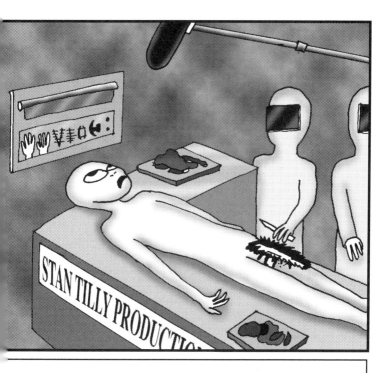

Zeynolds took up bit parts in snuff movies to supplement his income, and break into Hollywood.

Samantha from York was soon to realise she really should have listened to 'our Graham'.

hilst contemplating his own existence within the boundaries
his conscious mind, Zarax began to wonder whether the pills
Majax had given him at the club were such a good idea...

Pitch Invasion? Man, did they get the wrong end of that stick...!

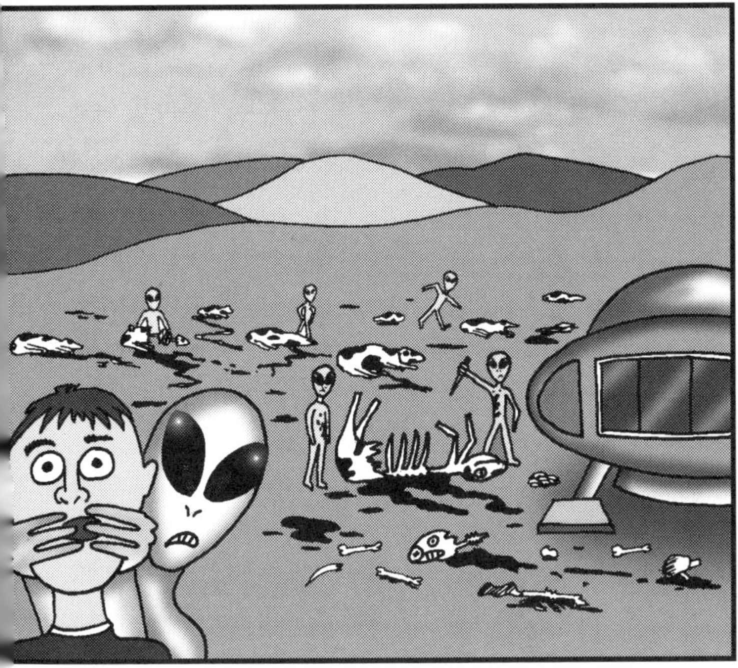

"The Boy Who Cried Alien."

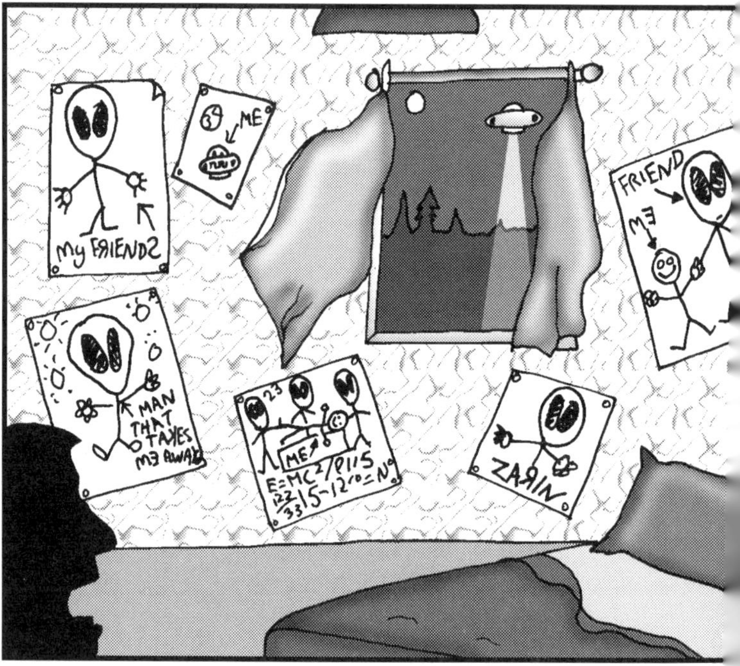
My FRIENDS
ME
FRIEND
ME
MAN THAT TAKES ME AWAY
ME
ZARIN

"Tommy...?"